This book belongs to

_____

DOUBLEDAY

New York   London   Toronto
Sydney   Auckland

THE BOY of the BELLS

WRITTEN BY CARLY SIMON

ILLUSTRATED BY MARGOT DATZ

PUBLISHED BY DOUBLEDAY

a division of Bantam Doubleday Dell Publishing Group, Inc.
666 Fifth Avenue, New York, New York 10103

DOUBLEDAY and the portrayal of an anchor
with a dolphin are trademarks of Doubleday,
a division of Bantam Doubleday Dell
Publishing Group, Inc.

Designed by Marysarah Quinn

Library of Congress Cataloging-in-Publication Data
Simon, Carly.
The boy of the bells/Carly Simon: illustrated by Margot Datz.—
—1st ed.
p. cm.
Summary: A young boy, with a little advice from Santa Claus,
performs a miracle on Christmas Day, restoring joy to his
sister's heart.
[1. Christmas—Fiction. 2. Brothers and sisters—Fiction.
3. Miracles—Fiction.] I. Datz, Margot, 111. II. Title.

ISBN 0-385-41587-7

Text copyright © 1990 by Carly Simon

Illustrations copyright © 1990 by Margot Datz

*To my son Ben and to his
grandfathers, Richard and Isaac*
—C.S.

*To my son Charlie IV and to his
grandfathers, Charles J. Blair II
and Edward E. Datz*
—M.D.

In a small village very far up north, there lived a grandfather and his two grandchildren. The village was called Noël, because from September all the way to April, it felt like Christmas there. Indeed, Noël was the first stop on Santa's well-mapped voyage around the world. In October the townspeople of Noël began making Christmas

wreaths out of the wildflowers and pine still fresh and sweet after the short months of summer. By early November, nearly every house had a decorated Christmas tree, and snow Santas, of all shapes and sizes, sat plump and frozen in front yards and on porches.

Grandfather Juniper and his two grandchildren, Miranda and Ben, lived in a little house attached to the village church where Grandfather Juniper's job was to mark time by ringing the bells in the steeple from six in the morning until midnight. He had been doing this for fifty-three years. But this Christmas, Grandfather was tired and worried about Miranda. His concern had begun one morning last winter when Miranda joined Ben and Grandfather for breakfast, but had said not one word. They ignored it at first, explaining her silence as sleepiness or maybe a bad mood, but even now, these many months later, it continued. She seemed to hear everything, and though she often smiled sweetly in response to her teacher's questions or Ben's funny jokes, she never uttered a sound. No one could figure it out, not even the village doctor, who examined her with his stethoscope and knee-jerking hammer. She who loved to sing didn't sing anymore. Mostly she sat in her room with her books, or made sketches of the pine trees draped with snow outside her window. She cooked the family's meals but sat silently while Ben and Grandfather tried in vain to get her to say even one word. Ben felt he had lost his best friend.

Christmas Eve was but one short night away. Because

Grandfather was so weary, he asked Ben, only ten years old, to take his place in the belfry. Ben felt honored to ring the bells on such a special night. He always enjoyed watching his grandfather pull the big cord which made the bell ring, allowing a sound like no other to fill the air. He had slowly learned the technique from his grandfather, but only recently were his arms strong enough to pull sufficiently hard on the rope.

Christmas Eve arrived with a moonless sky. A strong west wind piled snow high up on the windowpanes. Miranda was making a hearty Christmas soup and neighbors had brought fresh bread and plum pudding into Grandfather Juniper's kitchen. The red candles were lit, and a fire in the hearth cast a warm and comforting glow on the visitors.

"Here's to the merriest Christmas yet," said Jonathan the baker, as he lifted his glass of cranberry punch. "And here's to young Ben's first night alone in the bell tower."

"Take a blanket and pillows with you, and maybe some plum pudding in case you get hungry," his grandfather said, sending him off with a smile.

"Merry Christmas, Ben!" said all his rosy-faced friends.

Miranda just looked at her brother and blew him a kiss.

Ben climbed up the spiral staircase to the tower. There were thirty-two steps. They were crooked, and most of them had squeaks and creaks. He checked his watch: six minutes before eight o'clock. His heart was filled with pride and excitement as he settled into Grandfather Juniper's big comfortable chair.

"Am I really going to meet Santa Claus?" he wondered. "What will he think when he sees *me* instead of Grandfather?" He took the rope in his hands and at exactly eight o'clock he rang the big bell. It sounded crisp and melodious as it rang through the little village. Children all over Noël heard it and readied themselves for bed. Stockings were hung and parents kissed and cookies and milk left on kitchen tables. Lights dimmed in the windows of the sleepy town.

By the time Ben rang the ten o'clock bell, the town was hushed and the fires were out. Ben wondered if Miranda was still awake listening to him sound the chimes. Was she proud, was she excited? Ben wished he knew. He wanted his sister to be happy. He wanted her to speak again and care again and sing again and be lively and talk and talk and talk and TALK!

Then Ben had an idea. What if he sounded the bell *twelve* times at eleven o'clock? Then maybe Santa would get to Noël an hour early and Ben would have a chance to talk to him and explain about Miranda's silence. Maybe Santa could help! He thought about his plan and said to himself: "Yes! This is so important. Santa will understand."

At eleven o'clock Ben took the heavy cord in his hands and pulled it hard and with confidence. Twelve times the bell rang through the night. Then he sat back down in the chair and waited. The only sound was the wind blowing the fine flakes of snow against the west window of the tower.

Up at the North Pole, Santa woke from a deep sleep and thought: "Something is odd."

"What is this?" said Santa. "Am I growing so old and tired that I don't hear my wife call my name?" But then he looked over and saw that Mrs. Claus was just as surprised as he was.

"Oh dear, hurry, Nicholas," she urged. "I'll help you dress. I guess our alarm clock must be broken. There *were* twelve chimes from Noël, I'm sure of it." Santa mumbled awake, donned his red suit, grabbed a biscuit and mounted his sleigh. His reindeer were quite confused by this rapid departure.

"Good reindeer! Don't worry, my friends, we'll make up some time over the ocean. The wind's from the west, we're in luck!" He blew a kiss to Mrs. Claus and took off in a swirl of strong winds, snow and confusion.

In but a minute or two they were in Noël. Santa parked his sleigh in the sky by the clock tower and entered the warm room usually occupied by his good friend Juniper. He was surprised to see Ben instead. Ben wasted no time explaining.

"Oh, Santa, I struck the bells an hour early because I have to talk to you. Grandfather asked me to take over

because he was tired...You see, he's terribly worried about Miranda, ah, that's my sister...She hasn't talked in almost a year and we don't know why...We're all so upset about it and I'm lonely because she's my best friend and gosh, I really hoped you might be able to make her talk again." Ben said this excitedly, all in one breath, as he looked up into Santa's eyes and saw an expression that was nearly the opposite of a twinkle. He was afraid to name it.

"Santa, I hope I haven't made you angry with me."

"You know, Ben, your grandfather gave you a big job. All year I wait for those bells. All year I work hard making my sack of toys and sleigh ready for just this night..." Santa frowned at Ben, obviously very annoyed. His face was definitely not merry or rosy, and in fact his belly looked a little less robust than in pictures.

"Oh dear," Ben said. "I guess I didn't think hard enough about it."

"There are many children all over the world who have problems. But I don't have a magic wand to make their troubles disappear. No, Ben, this is your challenge." Santa was stern, but a gentle understanding was not far from creeping back into his crinkly eyes.

"I'm so sorry, Santa. I was only trying to help Miranda. Don't leave anything for me this year. But please, is there anything you can explain to me about Miranda's silence?"

"I'm sorry about your sister, Ben," said Santa. "But I can't always tell you why some things happen the way they do. There are many mysteries in the universe. I can tell you why it stays so cold in the North Pole most of the year, but I can't tell you why I get a warm feeling of excitement all down my back when I hear a church bell ring. But one thing we learn in the North Pole is to do the very best job—just for today—that we ourselves can do."

"Just for today?" asked Ben, uncertainly.

"Listen well, son." Santa stroked his whiskers and put his arm around Ben's shoulder.

"Yes, Santa?" said Ben, ready to take on the most impossible task.

"When you wake the town this morning, ring the bells as if you were the greatest musician on Earth. Make each stroke count. Invent sounds you've never heard before. Reach deep down inside you for inspiration. Make your grandfather proud."

As Santa turned to go, he looked back at Ben and said: "This is just between you and me. Right, Ben?"

"Thank you, Santa." Ben blew Santa a kiss. Santa's eyes lit up with Santa light and glowed like two fire opals beneath his snow-white eyebrows. Off he disappeared and Ben heard only the faint ringing of sleigh bells as Santa and his reindeer sailed up and then farther up into the snowy Christmas night.

Maybe it was just good luck or the way the wind was blowing or the way the snow was drifting or the way the pines were swaying, but no one at all in the town of Noël

was awake to hear the bells toll a second time, at the actual stroke of midnight. Some children murmured and shifted position under their comforters. Some grown-ups had dreams about when they were children. Miranda dreamed of a little house by the sea where the cries of sea gulls announced the hours of the day as they streamed through the blue summer skies. Grandfather Juniper dreamed of Ben holding a great silver baton and conducting an orchestra in the sky.

But Ben was not even a little bit tired. He was planning a feast. A feast of sounds.

Forty or more dusty bells, gongs and chimes of every kind that Grandfather had used over the years were stacked up all around the floor and shelves of the bell tower. Between midnight and one o'clock Ben dusted them all, tried each one for tone and pitch, and assembled them in a row. Ben chose a small bell to peal the first hour of Christmas morning. After all, he didn't want to wake anyone. At two, three, four and five in the morning, Ben added more and more bells, learning about their magical sounds as he tried each one.

And then, as the sky began to brighten in the east, as the snow tapered off to a flurry and as the wind softened to a whisper, Ben gathered his instruments beside him: his sticks, mallets and hammers in his hands, his gongs, bells and chimes spread out in front of him. It was close to six o'clock. Ben was tired but not tired, he was excited but calm, he felt chilly but somehow on fire. He wanted Grandfather to be proud and Santa to forgive him.

Listening to a quiet voice inside him, a voice more like music than words, Ben began to ring the bells. He was open to the songs of all the heavens. It was a symphony of bells. Chimes from India and Africa, gongs from China and Iceland, bells from all over the world sounded together, an ocean of bells.

Gusty blasts of music filled the morning air and woke the dreamers. Boys and girls all over Noël ran to the hearths where they had hung their stockings the night before. Parents and grandparents, aunts and uncles pleaded for a few more minutes of warmth and quiet before leaving their beds to start their wood fires and put on the coffee. But everyone, absolutely everyone, could hear the magic coming from the bell tower in the center of the village. Maybe it lasted one minute, maybe more like ten, but the symphony of bells remained in everyone's memory for the rest of their lives.

Ben was so thrilled he could have kept on ringing the bells all morning, but he heard something that made him pause. He heard footsteps on the stairs leading up to the bell tower. They creaked slow and steady, soft and feminine.

"Ben. Ben?" Miranda appeared, a glimmering figure in the doorway. Ben stopped and turned in surprise.

"Ben, that's the most beautiful sound I've ever heard! I really thought I was dreaming. I can't believe it's you!" Miranda laughed and a ray of sunlight made her presence even more dazzling. Her eyes shone with joy as they hadn't for months, which made tears come to Ben's eyes.

"Miranda, I'm so happy! Merry Christmas, it's so good to *hear* you again!"

"Merry Christmas, Ben. C'mon, let's go downstairs, make breakfast and open our presents."

Ben followed his sister down the rickety stairs, but he looked to the sky as he descended.

"Thank you, Mr. Santa Claus," he said in a whisper, and he imagined Santa's face before him. For a second or two, he was sure he heard Santa's sleigh bells and Santa seemed to be saying:

"It was you, Ben, it was all you…"

THE END